TWO TEEN VAMPIRES!

Adapted by Natalie Shaw

Simon Spotlight

New York London Toronto Sydney New Delhi

SIMON SPOTLIGHT

An imprint of Simon & Schuster Children's Publishing Division

1230 Avenue of the Americas, New York, New York 10020

This Simon Spotlight edition August 2018

TM & © 2018 Sony Pictures Animation Inc. All Rights Reserved.

All rights reserved, including the right of reproduction in whole or in part in any form.

SIMON SPOTLIGHT and colophon are registered trademarks of Simon & Schuster, Inc.

For information about special discounts for bulk purchases, please contact Simon & Schuster Special Sales at 1-866-506-1949 or business@simonandschuster.com.

Manufactured in the United States of America 0718 LAK

10 9 8 7 6 5 4 3 2 1

ISBN 978-1-5344-2640-5 (hc)

ISBN 978-1-5344-2639-9 (pbk)

ISBN 978-1-5344-2641-2 (eBook)

Toward the end of that summer I was coming home from a swimming pool in Little Italy, about a mile away, where kids could swim for a penny. I remember that my swimming suit was still wet under my clothes and that I took a short cut across the Northwestern tracks. There was a long board fence bounding the coalyard there, in those years, and as I passed a place where a board was missing a kid poked his head out and hissed, "Hey, you, c'mere," as though he'd been expecting me. I'd never seen the kid before. He was about seven, I guess.

He squatted down in the weeds and came up with a green bandanna in which lay eight singles and some small change. "That's your part," he tells me, and gives me half the bills and half the change. He'd taken it all out of a Northwestern caboose, and he knew it was stealing as well as I. That was why he'd called me: to share his guilt.

Only, I didn't feel guilty. I'd already had my beating for stealing so what I had in my hand had been well paid for. I felt as though somebody, maybe God, had owed me this for a long time and it was only in the natural run of things that it should come my way at last. And as I stood there the warmth of the coins, that had been lying in summer sunlight, spread from my palm through my whole body; for Aunt's warmth was in all coins. When I closed my fist over them I was enclosing her hand, and in that moment they became so precious to me that my fingernails dug into the flesh as if I never wanted to open my hand again. Then I thought of the old man and flattened the bills and stuffed them into my rolled sleeves. I don't know where I got the idea to do that, but kids raised on crowded corners get cunning pretty early.

I wandered around looking for kids I knew and found half a dozen ragged strays lagging beer corks on the corner of Allen Street. With a prissy-looking eleven-year-old blonde watching in solemn disapproval. I knew her. She lived next door and spent half her life, it seemed to me, on the alert for me to do something wrong in order to report it to the old man. If I spent a penny a mile away she'd learn of it and I'd become entangled in such a web of lies, trying to duck another beating, that I wouldn't know myself what the truth was.

So I stood there, with the most money I'd ever had in my life and just as unable to buy anything with it as though all the ice-cream parlors had closed for keeps. My bathing suit began to itch.

Kids are sly all right. There wasn't any use waiting for her to leave. She'd find out anyhow. So when no one was looking I dropped a dollar in the dirt and hollered, "Oh boy! Look what I found!" The lagging stopped.

"Augie found a dollar! We were all here'n nobody seen it but Augie! Augie the lucky eagle-eye!"

So here we all go to the ice-cream store, with the kids crowding around me and the prissy blonde following like a little Pinkerton. I bought two cones for myself first and alternated at licking them—one chocolate and one vanilla. I didn't like strawberry even then.

I don't think all the kids got cones, because there must have been at least forty swarming into the store by that time.

The blonde got one though. A strawberry double-header.

When the lagging was resumed and the excitement had subsided I felt a crying need for more ice cream.

It was getting toward suppertime but I hated going home, even to rid myself of the itching bathing suit; I felt a couple more cones would keep me going to all hours.

This time I played it safe. I only used a half dollar, which seemed then only half as wrong.

"Look! A halfer! Am I lucky today you!"

"Is he lucky today you. Lucky Augie the eagle-eye!"

And so back to the ice-cream store.

When I came out of the house the next morning half a dozen kids were waiting for me. Kids I'd never seen before from way over on Chicago Avenue. They didn't say anything, but they followed me so closely it was impossible to lose a penny without being seen in the act. And, of course, the twenty-four-hour Pinkerton, the eye that never slept, a little taller than any of the other kids, still shadowing me and still as grave as ever.

The sprouts followed my very eyes: if I glanced toward a telephone pole they would race there and search the alley for yards around. The blonde didn't search. She was hep. She just watched my pockets and my hands.

It didn't do her any good, because I started lagging beer corks with the other kids until her interest wandered to other suspects on whom she was keeping book. And that evening I *earned* seventy-five cents selling the *Saturday Evening Blade* on the corner of Milwaukee Avenue and Ashland.

The same kids were waiting for me the next morning, and I spent every dime of the *Saturday Evening Blade* money on them before noon, to maintain my far-flung reputation as an easy spender. Six bits in a single morning broke all local records for loose living.

And you can guess the rest: as soon as she'd finished another strawberry double-header the Pinkerton raced to Ma. "Augie steals money every day," she told the old lady.

"A lot you got to holler, Sissie," I told her. "You helped me spend it." I knew it wasn't any use saying I'd earned it selling the *Blade*. It was a beating either way.

Every time I was whipped unjustly I became lonely for Aunt, and the next morning I started out looking for her, to tell her how it was that nobody bothered you when you spent stolen money, except to help you spend it; but that the pay-off came when you were caught spending money you'd earned honestly. I couldn't figure that out, beyond feeling that my mistake had been in going to work at all. If I'd gone searching around that broken board in the coalyard fence, it seemed to me, instead of fooling around with the *Blade,* I might have done better. At least I wouldn't have been licked.

I had no idea where she lived, and so just wandered around looking at houses and occasionally ringing a doorbell in some blind hope that that might be the place she lived. I knew better than to ask Ma where Aunt lived, because all Ma did when I mentioned Aunt was to bawl.

It got so late that I was afraid to go home without some excuse. I'd been up and down streets and alleys the whole morning and most of the afternoon. And now the red headlines of the *Blade,* which had been featuring kidnap stories, came to my mind. Toward dark I stopped in an alley, found a piece of glass, and gave myself a long scratch down my right arm. The

CHAPTER ONE

The moment Mavis had been waiting for was finally here. She was watching her favorite rock star, Jett Black, on a TV in the Hotel Transylvania lobby when the mail arrived. A zombie bellhop hurried over, growled something, and held up an envelope. Mavis knew what was inside without even having to open it.

"They're here! They're finally here!" Mavis yelled to no one in particular as she waved the envelope in the air. "Tickets to Jett Black at the Roachella Batcave. This is going to rock!"

Roachella was the coolest rock concert in all eternity, and Mavis had written a song that was going to be performed by Jett Black. As Mavis cheered and danced around the lobby, she didn't notice Aunt Lydia, her father's sister, walking in.

"Too bad you can't go," Aunt Lydia said, snatching the tickets out of Mavis's hands . . . and staying true to her habit of always taking the fun out of everything. "Look at how busy we are!" Aunt Lydia waved her arms in a dramatic arc, but her words echoed through the lobby . . . because the only other monster in sight was a giant cricket hotel guest sitting by the fireplace.

"Cricket. Cricket," it chirped, making the lobby feel even emptier than it already was.

"Um, it looks sort of slow to me," Mavis said matter-of-factly.

"Slow?" Aunt Lydia replied. "The zombies are due for rot-proofing, the Cerberus is about to have puppies, and Quasimodo's staff is home sick with *being dead*. Besides, pop music is atrocious. It ages

me something awful. You will not attend that show!"
Aunt Lydia didn't even wait to see how Mavis would
respond before leaving the lobby.

Mavis was furious. She couldn't believe that her
aunt wasn't going to let her go to the concert because
of a few teeny, tiny problems at the hotel.

Mavis stomped out of the lobby and down a
hallway. "Aunt Lydia is so out of touch! Talk about a

drama queen!" Mavis said to herself as she paced back and forth, first on the floor and then on the ceiling. "I wish there was a way to make her feel young again. Then I bet she'd love Jett as much as I do!"

That was when she heard a clanging sound coming from behind a dungeon door. It was coming from Uncle Gene's workshop.

CHAPTER TWO

Inside, Uncle Gene was using a contraption with a spray nozzle to put zombie body parts back together.

"Mavis, my little poison spider egg, how are you?" Uncle Gene asked.

Mavis shrugged. "Same old, same old. Aunt Lydia is ruining my afterlife," she said. Then she pointed at the sprayer. "What's this?"

"I'm setting up a zombie sprayer," Uncle Gene said. He explained that the zombie sprayer was full of anti-rot serum that kept things from decaying. "It's just in time, too," he said as a stretcher full of zombie body parts, carried in by two zombies, fell apart, and everything tumbled to the ground.

As the zombie heads rolled, Uncle Gene told Mavis more about the serum. "It slows decomposition by reversing the aging process. It's also great on rotten egg salad."

He held up a tray of rotten egg salad to demonstrate. He sprayed it with anti-rot serum, and in seconds, the rotten eggs looked fresh again!

"Hold up," Mavis said excitedly. "That stuff reverses aging?"

"Well, since zombies are already dead, it only stops them from falling apart. But technically, if you sprayed a monster, it would grow back an old arm," Uncle Gene said. As he talked, he sprayed the serum on a zombie who was split in two. The top and bottom halves of the zombie fused together. Whole again, the zombie walked off.

"You don't say?" Mavis said, getting what seemed to her like a very good idea. Then, when her uncle wasn't looking, Mavis grabbed a bottle of serum and held it behind her back.

"Well, good luck, Uncle Gene! See ya!" Mavis said as she ran out of the room, trying to act naturally so he wouldn't suspect anything, and failing.

Uncle Gene noticed that Mavis had taken a bottle and yelled a warning. "Stuff's only been tested on zombies, and I don't think even they know the long-term effects."

But Mavis was already gone.

CHAPTER THREE

Late that night, Mavis and her friends—Hank, Wendy, and Pedro—stood outside Aunt Lydia's bedroom. Mavis had put a spray-bottle top on the bottle of serum so it looked a bit like a perfume bottle.

"Mavis, I don't know if this is a good idea," Hank said.

"What? It's the *best* idea! Aunt Lydia's 'new perfume' will make her feel younger, she'll understand our situation, and Jett Black, here we come."

"Do we even know what this stuff smells like?" asked Wendy.

Pedro smiled. "I put a dead rat in there to spice it up," he said proudly.

Dead rat smell was Aunt Lydia's favorite scent. It seemed Mavis's plan just might work after all. Mavis quickly knocked on Aunt Lydia's door before anyone else could try to talk her out of it.

Aunt Lydia swung it open, vampire fangs bared,

looking even scarier than usual.

"Aunt Lydia!" Mavis tried very hard to sound cheery. "We just wanted to give you this . . . token of appreciation."

Aunt Lydia wasn't usually easily fooled, and this was no exception.

"I knew you were desperate to see your disgusting show, but I did not expect you would stoop to bribery." Aunt Lydia grabbed the bottle out of Mavis's hands and sniffed.

She raised an eyebrow. "However, you obviously put a great deal of thought into this gesture. So I accept your gift."

With that, Aunt Lydia took the serum and slammed the door.

Soon, the kids all fell asleep, huddled together outside Aunt Lydia's door. The next morning they were jolted awake by the shrunken head hanging from

Aunt Lydia's door handle. "Wake up!" it screamed.

Mavis quietly opened the door to Aunt Lydia's room, and they all crept inside.

Like most vampires, Aunt Lydia slept in a closed casket. As Mavis tried to wake Aunt Lydia, Hank spotted the serum bottle on the dresser. It was completely empty!

"You guys! She used the whole thing!" he said in a loud whisper.

Mavis was worried. She hadn't paid much attention to Uncle Gene's warning, but now she started to wonder if that was a horrible mistake. She reached out her hand toward the coffin and said softly, "Aunt Lydia, are you okay in there?"

In a flash, the coffin lid flew open, and Aunt Lydia popped up. Except it wasn't Aunt Lydia as Mavis had ever seen her: this Lydia looked younger, almost as if she were Mavis's age! "Wazzup!" Aunt Lydia yelled, sending the kids running out of the room and screaming in terror.

Aunt Lydia was confused. "What's their dealio?" she asked aloud. Then she cupped her hand over her mouth and tried to smell her own breath. It didn't smell great. "Ahh . . . coffin breath." Aunt Lydia sighed.

Mavis and the gang gathered by the front desk in the hotel lobby. They had turned Aunt Lydia into a teenager, and now they were convinced that she was going to be furious at them, as usual.

"I thought that stuff would just make her feel younger, not turn her into a teenager! She's gonna kill us! She's totally gonna kill us!" Mavis yelled.

"You're all gonna die," Aunt Lydia yelled at them from up on a balcony, "when you see my killer breakfast outfit!"

To everyone's surprise, Aunt Lydia didn't seem mad, and she looked *awesome*. She even smiled as she jumped onto the balcony ledge to show off her new clothes. She was wearing a black top with a sweetheart neckline, and a cute purple miniskirt over purple tights and black, knee-high, lace-up boots.

In the hotel's restaurant, Aunt Lydia even joined in the fun as the gang ate a massive worm sundae.

"Old Lydia would never let us do anything like this!" Hank said, and then realized calling her "Old Lydia" wasn't the nicest thing to say. "I mean . . . ," he began, but before he could make things worse, Mavis shoved a spoonful of worm sundae into his mouth.

"Say, Aunt Lydia, seeing as you're in such a youthful mood," Mavis began slowly. Then she blurted out her question as fast as she could:

"Can-we-have-our-tickets-back-pretty-please-so-we-can-go-see-Jett-Black-tonight-at-Roachella?"
Aunt Lydia looked up from her worm sundae.

"Hmm, I'm not sure. I can't think when I'm not throwing stuff into an abyss," she said. Then she ordered everyone to "go to the secret bottomless pit!"

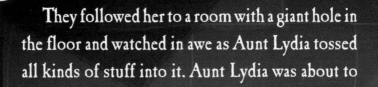

They followed her to a room with a giant hole in the floor and watched in awe as Aunt Lydia tossed all kinds of stuff into it. Aunt Lydia was about to toss the shrunken head from her bedroom door into the hole, but then paused and gave it to Mavis instead.

"Wait! I just thought of something else to chuck in! Be right *bat*," Aunt Lydia said, making a silly pun before running off.

Mavis was worried, but Wendy just tossed stuff into the hole while they waited for Aunt Lydia to return.

"I can't believe how great this worked out!" Wendy said.

"Actually, I'm starting to think it's working a little *too* well," Mavis confessed. Aunt Lydia's rules were annoying, but now Mavis realized they were kind of important.

"Ya *think?*" said the shrunken head, still in Mavis's hands. "With nobody in charge, the hotel will fall apart!"

Pedro thought the shrunken head was worrying too much. "She's got this under control. Right, Mavis?"

Just then, Aunt Lydia returned, dragging a giant block of granite. As she lifted it over her head to throw it into the hole, Mavis recognized it as an ancient vampire artifact, and gasped. "Aunt Lydia, stop! That's Vlad the Annoyer's scream stone! It's been in the family since forever!"

Aunt Lydia didn't seem to care. "Are you serious?" she asked, but then she shrugged and put the stone down. "Okay. Let's go find some real trouble to get into!"

Mavis tried to act cool as everyone else also shrugged and followed Lydia. She lingered for a moment and stared at the stone.

"I wonder why they call this the scream stone," Mavis said after the others left.

The face carved into the scream stone glared at Mavis, opened its mouth, and let out a very loud, very annoying, scream. "AAAAAAH-HHHHHHHHH!"

"Seriously?" Mavis said, covering her ears. She couldn't believe she had stepped in to save it, even if it was an heirloom. Without a moment's hesitation, she pushed the scream stone into the bottomless pit.

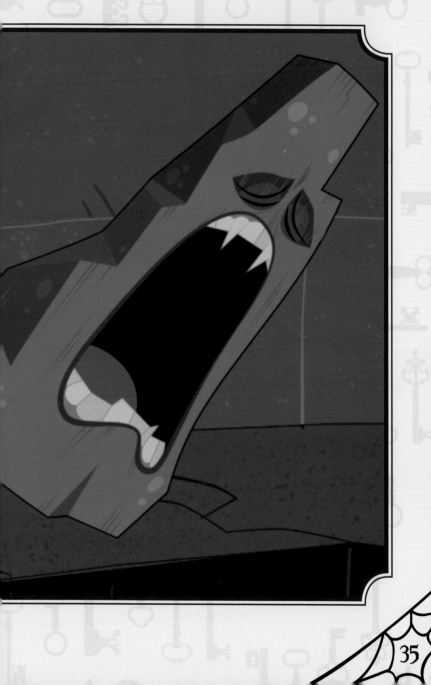

CHAPTER FOUR

Mavis couldn't find Aunt Lydia and the gang anywhere in the hotel. The lobby was empty, and it was a mess. Luggage was strewn all over the steps leading up to the front desk.

"You guys?" she yelled, hoping her friends would hear her. When there was no answer, she stopped and looked around. "Where did they go off to? Does anyone *work* here anymore?"

That was when Quasimodo, the chef, showed up. He was clutching his hand, which was covered in a bandage.

"Quasi? What happened to your hand?" Mavis asked.

"I got a paper cut from the recipe book!" Quasi

said. He made a big show of crying, as if he were in a lot of pain, to get Mavis's sympathy . . . but Mavis was not buying it. When he saw her scowling at him, he stopped crying. "Ah, you don't care," he said, and he was right.

"A paper cut? Back to work!" she ordered Quasi. She turned to a group of zombies who were lounging at the front desk and yelled at them too. "All of you, back to work! If you've got an arm, you can carry a bag."

Mavis couldn't believe what was happening at the

hotel. It seemed like nobody could figure out how to do anything without Aunt Lydia telling them what to do.

That's when she saw Aunt Lydia, Pedro, Hank, and Wendy tiptoeing across the lobby.

"Whoa, whoa, whoa!" Mavis shouted. "Where do you think you're going?"

Aunt Lydia pushed the others through the revolving

door before Mavis could stop her, and then she turned to Mavis. "Jett Black! Remember?"

Mavis couldn't believe what she was hearing. "But those are *my* tickets!" she said.

"You'll cover for us, right?" Aunt Lydia said as if nothing was wrong. "Don't wait up."

That was the last straw. Mavis was starting to feel like the grown-up around Hotel Transylvania, and it wasn't anywhere near as fun as being a kid. She didn't get a chance to tell her aunt though, because Aunt Lydia had slipped through the revolving door and down the stairs outside the hotel. Mavis went outside and shook her fist as she yelled in the direction her aunt and friends had gone.

"How can she be so irresponsible?" Mavis shouted. "Do you all think I can do everything around here myself? Look at how—" Mavis stopped midsentence as she came to a sudden realization. "Ohmi*goblin*, I'm Aunt Lydia!"

CHAPTER

FIVE

Mavis was right. She was becoming a lot like her aunt. She ran to Uncle Gene's workshop in the dungeon to see if he could help her. When she walked in, he was pushing a garbage bin full of zombie body parts.

Mavis explained what happened, and that Aunt Lydia was a teenager again. "I just really wanted to see Jett do my song," Mavis confessed, "but with Aunt Lydia goofing off, everything here is falling apart! You don't have some kind of serum that, like, speeds up aging, do you?"

Uncle Gene scoffed. "A serum to speed up aging?" he said as he popped a spare eyeball back into a zombie's face. Then he picked up two zombie arms and waved them around as he spoke. "Nope, only thing I've ever heard of like that is live pop music."

"Did you say 'live pop music'?" Mavis asked, her eyes opened wide with excitement.

"Oh sure. Rare allergy in certain vampires. Ages Lydia horribly."

"You're serious? I thought she was just being

a drama queen!" Mavis said, relieved. Then she squealed with excitement and ran over to give her uncle a hug. "That's it! Thanks, Uncle Gene! Looks like I'm going to Roachella after all!"

Mavis ran out of the room before Uncle Gene even noticed, which meant she didn't hear his warning... again.

"Of course, too much live rock music, and she'll turn to dust!" Uncle Gene said. "Happened to Cousin Camilla at a Mozart show back in 1783. That dude rocked *hard*."

Meanwhile, Mavis's friends were at the Roachella concert, which was held in a huge cave with a giant skull at the entrance. Inside, bats hung from the ceiling to watch the show upside down, and there was a large pool of water in between the stage and the audience.

As Mavis caught up with her friends and they went inside, Aunt Lydia showed up in a boat, and they all sailed together to their seats.

"Hey, look who finally learned the value of skipping work," Aunt Lydia teased Mavis.

"So, you're not mad?" Mavis asked cautiously.

"Nah, I don't care. Maybe *old* Lydia would care," Aunt Lydia said.

Mavis shrugged. "Well, we can ask her soon enough," she hinted.

Aunt Lydia asked Mavis what she meant by that strange sentence, but was interrupted by a loud bang and bright lights.

Jett Black was onstage . . . and he was rocking out!

Hearing the music, Aunt Lydia shrieked in pain. "Ow! What's going on?" she asked.

Mavis was happy to break the news to her aunt. She was ready for things to go back to normal again. "You're about to become Aunt Lydia again. And better yet, it's going to happen thanks to *my* song!"

Mavis began to sing along to Jett Black as he belted out her words:

> *Slug guts in my hair,*
> *Slug guts everywhere.*

Aunt Lydia covered her ears with her hands and dropped to the floor, writhing at the sound.

Wendy and Pedro looked concerned, so Mavis explained. "Aunt Lydia is allergic to pop music. Don't worry. . . . It's just aging her back to normal."

Aunt Lydia bent over in pain as her legs began to turn into dust, just as Uncle Gene had warned Mavis.

"Uh-oh! She's aging too far!" Mavis yelled to her friends.

Mavis needed to find a way to stop the music before Aunt Lydia was gone forever. She quickly turned into a bat, flew onstage, and then turned back into her vampire form so she could do the unthinkable: grab Jett Black's mellowtron—a musical instrument a bit like an electric guitar—and destroy it.

"Hey!" yelled Jett Black, but Mavis didn't listen. She smashed the mellowtron on the floor of the stage and broke it into pieces so the music would stop.

Then she picked up a big boulder from the cave floor and held it over her head.

"So, so, so, so, so, so sorry," she told a confused Jett Black, "but this is kind of an emergency." Then she rammed the boulder into the mellowtron to make sure it was really, really broken.

That last bit did the trick. "That's better!" Aunt Lydia said when the music stopped. She looked normal again, except that she was missing the bottom half of her body.

When Aunt Lydia looked down, she freaked out.

"What happened to my body?" she yelled.

Mavis didn't have time to explain. Jett Black walked up to her and shouted, "Mavis, you've totally ruined my comeback show!"

Mavis tried to make light of it all. "Song sounded great," she said weakly.

Jett Black wasn't happy. "I just want you to know that whenever I think back on the worst concert of my afterlife, I'll remember *that* face," he said, looking at her angrily.

Jett Black flew off, carried by flying monkeys.

Somehow, Wendy found a bright side to the whole thing.

"Did you hear that? Jett Black said he'll *always* remember you!" Wendy told Mavis, but that wasn't comforting at all.

Back at the hotel, Mavis watched as Uncle Gene used his zombie sprayer on Aunt Lydia. She quickly looked like her old self again—lower body and all.

Mavis ran over to her aunt and held up her hand to give her a high five, but Aunt Lydia left her hanging.

"I'm so glad you're okay!" Mavis said.

"Why are you trying to upper five me when there's work to be done?!" said Aunt Lydia.

"I know, and I'm sorry. I realize now that managing this place isn't a one-monster job," said Mavis.

"That is a very . . . grown-up lesson to have learned,

Mavis," Aunt Lydia said, actually smiling.

"So . . . I'm not going to be punished?" Mavis was hopeful.

"Of course you are," Aunt Lydia said as she walked to the door. "The scream stone needs to be polished."

"Oh no!" Mavis said, realizing that the scream stone was still falling in the bottomless pit . . . because she threw it there. This punishment might take the rest of her afterlife!